# Norman Bridwell
# CLIFFORD
# GOES TO WASHINGTON

## SCHOLASTIC INC.

New York   Toronto   London   Auckland   Sydney

Mexico City   New Delhi   Hong Kong   Buenos Aires

To
Leanna and T.J.
also
Lee and Tom
—N.B.

The author thanks Manny Campana
for his contribution to this book.

ISBN-13: 978-0-439-69656-2
ISBN-10: 0-439-69656-9

Copyright © 2005 by Norman Bridwell.
All rights reserved. Published by Scholastic Inc.
SCHOLASTIC, CARTWHEEL BOOKS, and associated logos are trademarks and/or registered trademarks of Scholastic Inc. CLIFFORD, CLIFFORD THE BIG RED DOG, and associated logos are trademarks and/or registered trademarks of Norman Bridwell.

Library of Congress Cataloging-in-Publication Data available.

12                                                                                      14/0
                                                                                          40

Do you have a dog? I do, and his name is Clifford.
I'm Emily Elizabeth.

Clifford has a lot of friends. One of his friends is Riley, a very good dog.

Not long ago, Riley did a very brave thing. He snatched a little kid out of the path of a car.

Riley's picture was in the paper, and he was on television.
Somebody in Washington, D.C., saw the news about Riley.

Riley was invited to the White House to receive a medal for his bravery.
Clifford was very happy for his friend.

Riley got to drive to Washington in a big car. Clifford wanted to see him get the medal, so he tagged along.

When we reached Washington, Riley's car crossed a river on a bridge.
Clifford was afraid he would break the bridge.

Clifford found another way.

It was a hot, sunny day, but some people thought it had started to rain.
The people in Washington, D.C., aren't used to having a big dog around.

Before we went to see Riley get his medal, Clifford
and I did some sightseeing.

Clifford's favorite statue was Abraham Lincoln.

Clifford also liked the statue of Thomas Jefferson.
Thomas Jefferson seemed to like Clifford, too.

Clifford was very excited to see the statue of Franklin Roosevelt's dog, Fala. Fala must have done some very great things to get his own statue.

Clifford and I saw a demonstration going on. The grass was filled with people carrying signs. Some were **for** something.

Some were **against** something. The people were all shouting.
Clifford found this very upsetting.

Then he had an idea. He gave them a place to get out of the heat.
Everyone enjoyed the shade and got along better.

I really wanted to go to the top of the Washington Monument, but the line was very long, and I didn't have enough time.

Clifford fixed that for me.

People were surprised to see a girl and a Big Red Dog way up there!

The view was breathtaking. But we couldn't stay long.
It was time for Riley to get his medal.

We rushed to the White House. We passed the National Aquarium.

And we raced by the Treasury Building.

We got to the White House just in time.
Riley and the First Lady were standing on the lawn.

Clifford was so happy to see Riley, he jumped over the fence.

A bunch of men in dark suits and sunglasses tried to tackle Clifford, but they couldn't do it.

Clifford thought he might be doing something wrong, so he sat down.
I explained to the men about Clifford and Riley being pals.

The First Lady told them to let Clifford stay.

She said, "We need people to be more like Clifford.
We need people to care about each other."

Then she gave Riley his medal.

And she gave Clifford a big hug.

That made our trip to Washington just perfect.

Good boy, Clifford!